WIMBLEDON

LIBRARY
HOLBEIN SCH.
MT. HOLLY, N.J.

Published by Creative Education, Inc.
123 South Broad Street, Mankato, MN 56001

Designed by Rita Marshall with the help of Thomas Lawton
Cover illustration by Rob Day, Lance Hidy Associates

Copyright © 1990 by Creative Education, Inc.
All rights reserved. No part of this book may be reproduced in any form without written permission from the publisher.

Photography by Allsport, Barry Rabinowitz,
Globe Photos, Hillstrom Stock Photo, Wide World Photos

Printed in the United States

Library of Congress Cataloging-in-Publication Data

Gilbert, Nancy.
 Wimbledon/by Nancy Gilbert: edited by Michael E. Goodman.
 p. cm.
 Summary: Explores the Wimbledon tennis competition from its beginnings to the present, discussing changes in rules and playing style and great players from Spencer Gore to Boris Becker.
 ISBN 0-88682-319-6
 1. All England Club—History—Juvenile literature. 2. Tennis players—Biography—Juvenile literature. [1. All England Club—History. 2. Tennis players.] I. Goodman, Michael E. II. Title.
GV997.A4G55 1989   89-29264
796.342′09422′1—dc20   CIP
                                                        AC

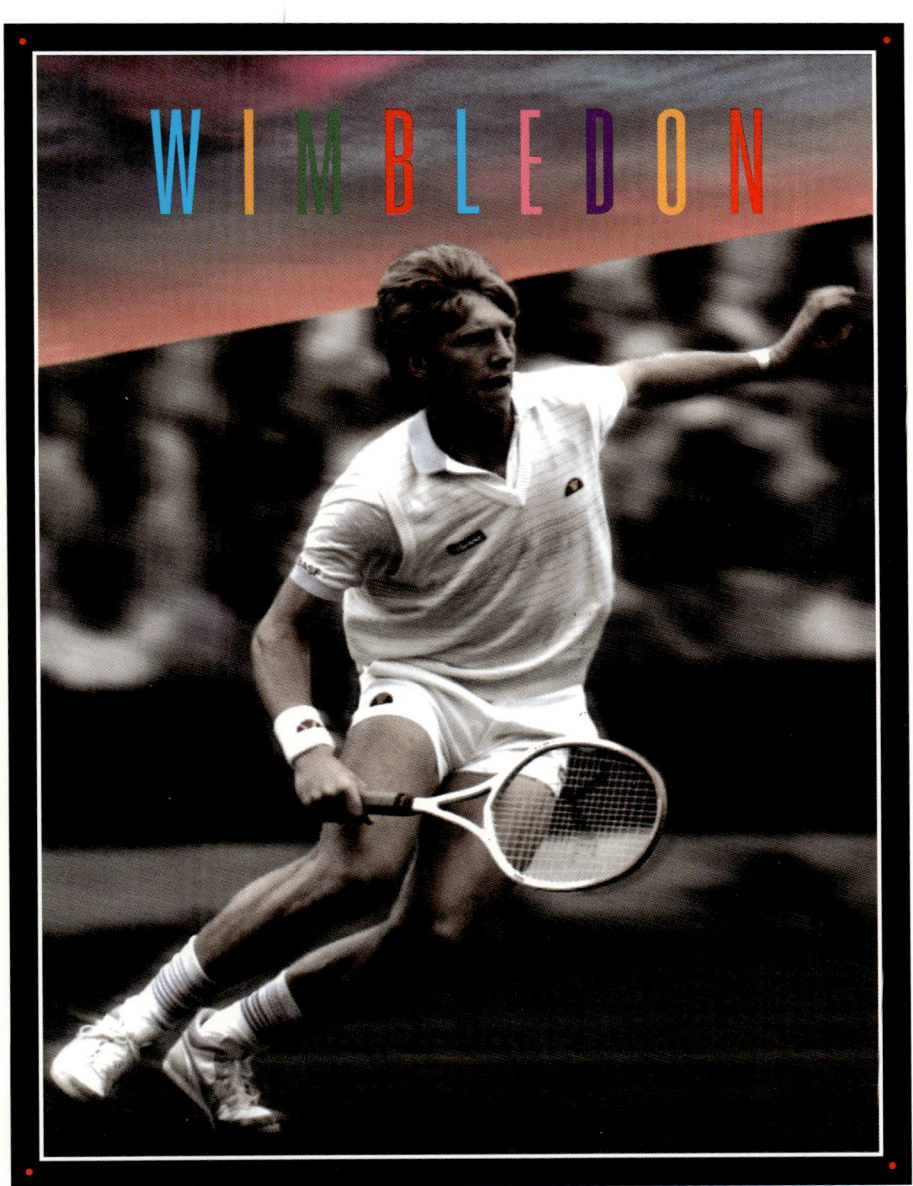

WIMBLEDON

NANCY GILBERT

CREATIVE EDUCATION INC.

Two weeks ago, a "fortnight," as they say in England, more than 100 of the finest tennis players in the world came to this spot in the suburbs of London, England, for a chance to be part of tennis history. Today, only two contestants remain. In a few minutes, the two will walk proudly, and a little nervously, onto the green grass of Centre Court.

Jimmy Connors and Bjorn Borg.

It is the most famous tennis court in the world and the richest in tennis tradition. There they will square off for the "All-England Championships"—better known as Wimbledon.

In the waiting room that leads to Centre Court, the two players wait nervously for the moment to come. As they wait, the players might thumb through a magazine, though they cannot concentrate on the words. They might sit on a couch that looks comfortable but isn't really. One might chatter, trying to settle his nerves. The other might stare off into space, pace around the room, or bite his lip.

They might be thinking of all the famous tennis players who have come before them to this place. Reminders of the game's legends are everywhere. On the way to the waiting room, they passed the wall on which the names of all the previous Wimbledon winners are listed. On the opposite wall, there are scattered photographs of past champions.

Finally, the referee comes to the waiting room to speak to the players and lead them to the court. Together they pass through the last pair of doors and enter Centre Court. The players stop to bow to members of the British royal family who sit in the royal box. Then they proceed to their chairs beside the referee's. No one introduces the players to the audience. It is assumed that everyone in the huge crowd knows who is about to play. A racket is spun to decide who will serve first and who will receive.

This is the men's singles finals of one of the most important tennis tournaments in the world. "There is only one Wimbledon," said 1920s star Bill Tilden. Women's tennis champion Billie Jean King seconded Tilden's thoughts: "There is a flavor about Wimbledon and a greatness that puts it on a pedestal by itself."

Like every other competitor, Boris Becker knows the importance of each Wimbledon match.

Jimmy Connors

For players and spectators alike, it is the traditions that make Wimbledon special. The matches are played on grass, the way tennis was played in the early days. The competitors wear "mostly white" when they play, as tennis players always did in the past.

But the traditions extend beyond the competition itself. Every year, more than 400,000 people come to the All-England Lawn and Tennis Club in Wimbledon during "the Fabulous Fortnight" in early summer. Once inside, most spectators make a day of it. They bring bag lunches or buy food at one of the concession stands. The traditional snack at Wimbledon is a bowl of strawberries and cream.

Many visitors take a few minutes to browse in the Wimbledon museum, which opened in 1977 for Wimbledon's 100th birthday. Among its fascinating exhibits are the championship trophies and a reconstruction of the players' dressing room as it looked during the first Wimbledon tournament in 1877.

But Championship Day is not for browsing. It is the time for tennis at its finest. The players' rocket serves race through the air and spin along the smooth grass surface at speeds of up to 150 miles per hour. They smash back service returns that travel almost as quickly. The players rush to the net to hit winning volleys. Or they hit spinning lobs that sail far above the head of their opponent and then touch down just inside the back court line for a winner.

Matches at Wimbledon are played on traditional grass courts.

Whose shots will be stronger and more accurate today? Whose overall game will be better? That person will still be unbeaten at the end of "the Fabulous Fortnight" and will wear the Wimbledon crown.

THE EARLY YEARS

Wimbledon is a major event today, but the tournament began as a much simpler affair in 1877. Three years before, a British army officer named Major Walter Clopton Wingfield had devised rules for a game that combined elements of court tennis, badminton, and rackets. He called his game Sphairistikè, a Greek word that means "ball game." No one could pronounce the name, so it soon became commonly known as "lawn tennis."

The sport grew rapidly in popularity. Eventually, the members of the All-England Croquet Club in Wimbledon decided to add tennis courts to the club grounds. By 1877, interest had grown so great that the club sponsored a men's singles tournament.

Twenty-two men entered this first Wimbledon championship. What occurred resembled the modern game of tennis somewhat but was different in many ways from what we see today. The rackets looked like snowshoes. The balls were hand sewn with flannel covers. The court was not rectangular; instead, it was shaped like an hourglass—narrower in the middle by the net and wider at the baselines. The net was five feet high at the sidelines, dipping to three feet in the middle. Today it is three feet, six inches high at the sidelines. Scoring was completely different, too. As in volleyball, only the server could earn a point.

This 1881 match differed greatly from the modern game of tennis.

Even the way the men played in that first tournament was very different from today. The players didn't really compete with each other and didn't care who won or lost. The server would put the ball in play with an underhand motion and wait at the baseline, the end of the court, for the return. That return was usually a gentle looping shot that was easy to return. It was considered bad sportsmanship to make the returner have to move very much to get to the ball. When a point was finally won, probably after one player became too tired to make a return, the loser would shout cheerily, "Jolly good stroke, old chap!"

Only one of the twenty-two players seemed to care about winning. He was Spencer Gore. Gore decided to "break the rules." He raced to the net on nearly every point and hit the ball before it bounced on the ground. Gore had thus invented the stroke known as the volley. His volleys quickly wiped out each opponent. With considerable ease, Gore became the first Wimbledon champion and gave all lawn tennis fans a great moment to remember.

By the 1880s, Wimbledon expanded to include women's and doubles competitions, along with men's singles. During that decade, the Renshaw twins, William and Ernest, dominated men's tennis at Wimbledon, capturing eight of the ten singles titles during the 1880s and seven of ten doubles crowns. The Renshaws added their own touches to the rules of lawn tennis. They invented the doubles style of having one player stay at the net while the other served the ball. The man at the net was thus in position to hit a winning volley when the opponents returned a serve. The Renshaws also were the first players to use an overhead smash shot to combat a lob.

Suzanne Lenglen used the overhead smash at Wimbledon in 1922.

Women's tennis also grew in popularity in the 1880s, and the All-England Club finally established a women's championship at Wimbledon in 1884. The first woman champion was Maud Watson, who won every match she played at Wimbledon or anywhere else between 1882 and 1886. Watson played by the old rules—she wore her opponents down by returning soft, looping baseline shots over and over again. The style lacked excitement but was effective.

Watson's winning streak ended when she met fifteen-year-old Charlotte "Lottie" Dod in the 1886 Wimbledon finals. Lottie was a great all-around athlete. She and her brothers were taught to play hard, in the style of the Renshaws. She charged the net and loved to hit volleys and overhead smashes. Using this aggressive style, she easily defeated Watson and every other opponent to win five Wimbledon titles. Six years after storming onto the tennis scene, Lottie Dod turned away from tennis at age twenty-one. She took up golf and soon became a British golf champion, too.

The Renshaws and Lottie Dod helped change tennis from a "gentlemanly" game to a strong competitive sport. They also helped transform Wimbledon from a gentle sporting event to an outstanding athletic competition that would provide tennis fans with many great moments in the years to come.

THE GOLDEN YEARS

At the turn of the century, new champions emerged and the tournament increased in size and popularity. By 1922 it had outgrown its home at the All-England Club and was moved to its present site in another part of the town of Wimbledon. The tournament prospered even more in its new home, and the period of the 1920s and 1930s has become known as "the Golden Years."

A century later, Steffi Graf displays the same aggressive style as Lottie Dod.

Players such as Helen Wills, Fred Perry, Bill Tilden, and Rene Lacoste displayed marvelous skill and provided great moments that will live on in Wimbledon history forever. But two particular players will be remembered for their behavior off the court as well as on it.

Rene Lacoste provided many great moments during "the Golden Years."

The first great women's star of the Golden Years was a young French woman named Suzanne Lenglen, who won at Wimbledon six times between 1919 and 1925. Suzanne's father decided when she was only eleven that she should be a tennis champion. He watched the best players and taught Suzanne the forehand of one top player, the backhand of another, and the serve of a third. When she made a stroke particularly well or directly hit a target he had placed on the court, he would give her a coin as a reward. He also had her skip rope daily, run sprints, and do other exercises to increase her strength and stamina. By the time she was thirteen years old, Lenglen was ready to compete in tournaments against the top women in France. Within two years, she was a star.

Like Lenglen before her, Martina Navratilova became a renowned champion in the 1970s.

When she was twenty, Lenglen went to England for her first Wimbledon. She was a sensation in England—and not only for her tennis skill. She also changed the way women dressed on the court. According to Lenglen's doubles partner Elizabeth Ryan, "All women tennis players should go down on their knees in thankfulness to Suzanne for delivering them from the tyranny of corsets." Before Lenglen, women tennis players had worn corsets and stiff petticoats, long sleeves, and loose collars on the court. Then in 1919, Lenglen shocked everyone when she appeared at Wimbledon wearing a one-piece, calf-length cotton dress with short sleeves. Her hair was cut short, and she wrapped a long band of silk around it.

Lenglen's outfit was not only exciting to look at; it was also practical. It made

Suzanne Lenglen created a sensation at Wimbledon.

it possible for her to move more easily than her opponent. But she didn't really need this advantage because her tennis playing was spectacular. She won the 1919 final over seven-time champion Dorothea Chambers in three tough sets, outlasting her opponent 9–7 in the last set. This was Suzanne Lenglen's first Wimbledon victory. She went on to win the women's singles crown five more times and also captured nine titles in women's doubles and mixed doubles, where a man and woman team together.

Lenglen played her last Wimbledon in 1926. She made it to the semifinals in both singles and doubles and was scheduled to play both matches on the same afternoon, with singles first. Tournament officials came to ask if she would mind playing the doubles match earlier. The Queen of England would be arriving later in the day and wished to watch her in the singles competition. Lenglen refused, noting that she needed the best light for the more important singles match. "If the Queen wishes to see me, she must arrive at the scheduled hour like everyone else," she said. The officials were angry with her attitude and forced her to drop out of the tournament. Lenglen refused to play Wimbledon ever again. The London papers attacked her "French temperament," but Lenglen would never take second place—even to a queen.

In the late 1930s, Don Budge became the top men's player in the world. He proved his greatness in 1938 when he won the Australian championship, the French championship, Wimbledon, and the United States championship—all in the same year. Budge thus became the first person to win tennis's "Grand Slam." Only one other man and four women have ever achieved this feat in tennis history.

Budge nearly blew his chance for the Grand Slam at Wimbledon. He was playing poorly and barely won his first two matches. His famous backhand shot seemed to have deserted him, and he was convinced that he would lose the next round. Budge went for a walk along the outer courts at Wimbledon, where some older women were playing. There, he watched one of the women hit a backhand with perfect spin. Budge rushed back to the dressing room and convinced a friend to practice with him for a few minutes. "Just hit it to my backhand," he told the friend. He returned every shot just as the woman had done. Budge's backhand was back. A few days later, Budge breezed through the finals with a 6–1, 6–0, 6–3 victory. His opponent told the press, "I have never seen such tennis as Don showed today." When he received the winner's trophy, Budge silently saluted the woman who had helped him regain his backhand and his confidence.

World War II brought an end to the Golden Years in 1939, but the period will always be remembered for the talent and personality of the great players who made the era such a glorious one in tennis history.

Lew Hoad was one of the top men's players in the 1960s.

FROM DOWN UNDER

The Golden Years may have concluded twenty years earlier, but the 1960s also had their share of great moments in Wimbledon history. For the most part, these were provided by the talented men and women of Australia. Rod Laver led the way, but there were others as well. Lew Hoad and Ken Rosewall starred on the men's side, and Margaret Court Smith and Evonne Goolagong dominated the women's competition.

Ivan Lendl used the same shot in the '80s that Budge made popular years before.

Boris Becker

Smith and Goolagong were very different from the wealthy socialites who had played at Wimbledon in its early days. Each came from a poor family and was a self-taught player. Each began playing when she was only nine years old. Smith grew up across the street from

a tennis club, and she used old balls that had been hit over the club's hedges and a long, thin board as her first racket. Goolagong came from a tiny village in the back country of Australia. She taught herself to play tennis, sending old balls over a rope she had strung across her backyard.

Evonne Goolagong won her first Wimbledon in 1971.

Despite their difficult beginnings, both women rose to the top of the tennis world. Smith became known for her powerful strokes that helped her capture Wimbledon titles in 1963, 1965, and 1970 and the Grand Slam in 1970. Her 1970 Wimbledon triumph over American Billie Jean King is considered one of the top matches ever in the great tournament. The two women, rated numbers one and two in the world at that time, battled evenly for nearly two and a half hours, the longest women's final in Wimbledon history. In the end, Smith won 14–12, 11–9, but not before King had saved five match points. The two stars left the court exhausted as the fans gave them a standing ovation.

The next year, Goolagong captured her first Wimbledon title. She also captured the hearts of the English fans with her special style and charm.

The English crowds at Wimbledon loved all of the Aussies, from Lew Hoad to Evonne Goolagong, even if they spoke English with a "funny" accent. They shared the same queen and the same love for the game born in England nearly 100 years before.

SWEDEN VS. AMERICA

By the late 1970s, the Aussie champs were replaced at Wimbledon by two rivals with very different playing styles and personalities. Bjorn Borg of Sweden was known as the "ice man" for his lack of emotion while playing and his crystal-hard ground strokes. Borg wore his opponents down by returning everything they hit at him. He never smiled, he never complained, and he almost never lost. Between 1976 and 1980, Borg won Wimbledon five times in a row.

By the mid-1970s, Bjorn Borg was Wimbledon's dominant men's player.

Borg's main rival in these years was John McEnroe, a bashing left-hander from Queens, New York. McEnroe sometimes pouted and yelled at umpires, and he was often booed loudly by the proper British fans, who thought that he should be more of a gentleman and less of a brat.

Borg and McEnroe met often at the finals of international tournaments in the late 1970s and early 1980s. But no match between them can compare with the Wimbledon final of 1980. The match was a thrilling spectacle, lasting three hours and fifty-three minutes. McEnroe depended on his hard, kicking serve and accurate volleys. Borg made good use of his outstanding two-handed backhand and his powerful top spin. Both players displayed the courage and determination to battle on through the long afternoon.

John McEnroe emerged as Borg's main rival.

The thrilling 1980 final lasted almost four hours.

McEnroe won the first set 6–1, but Borg took the next two. Then came the magnificent fourth set. Borg broke out on top and was leading 5–4 and serving for the match. Everyone thought he would win for sure. But the "ice man" had an attack of nerves, and his shots lost their zing. McEnroe saved two match points to even the set at 5 all.

At 6 all, they began the tiebreaker of the ages. A tiebreaker is a special type of game designed to speed up play. The first player to reach seven points wins the set. But the player must win by two points. This particular tiebreaker didn't save any time. It took twenty-two minutes, only five minutes less than the entire first set. First McEnroe had a chance to win the set when he went ahead 8–7, but Borg made a brilliant shot to even the tiebreaker. Then Borg went ahead and had his first of five match points, each of which McEnroe won. The two men scrambled and dived, hitting spectacular shots under the most intense pressure. McEnroe served for the set at 17–16. When Borg missed a forehand volley by inches, McEnroe took the set and evened the match.

McEnroe had a chance to win the set when he took the lead 8–7.

Another player with less confidence and concentration than Borg might have folded at that point. Instead, Borg held on to take the fifth set by a score of 8–6. Borg had won his fifth consecutive Wimbledon title. All who witnessed the match, the thousands in the stands and millions more on television, knew that they had seen one of the great tennis matches of all time.

BEATING THE ODDS

While Borg and McEnroe were battling on the men's side at Wimbledon, three women provided the thrills on the other side of the tournament. Billie Jean King, Chris Evert, and Martina Navratilova were the focus of attention from the 1970s to the early 1980s, winning championships and changing the face of women's tennis around the world. By the late 1980s, however, the great moments most remembered were provided by two young West Germans.

Seventeen-year-old Steffi Graf first burst upon the Wimbledon scene in 1987, losing a heartbreaking championship match to Navratilova. Since then, Graf has been virtually unbeatable. The following year she avenged her defeat to Navratilova, winning her first Wimbledon championship.

Chris Evert was a perennial champion during the 1970s and '80s.

But her greatest Wimbledon moment occurred in 1989. Coming back from an early one-set deficit, Graf rallied in the summer's heat to win the next two sets. She had won her second consecutive championship. When Graf raised the winner's silver plate over her head, it was clear that this could be a great moment that would be repeated many times.

In 1988, eighteen-year-old Steffi Graf won her first Wimbledon.

Steffi Graf was not the only teenage Wimbledon champ of the 1980s from West Germany. Her fellow countryman Boris Becker captured three titles in five years between 1985 and 1989.

Little-known Boris Becker became the youngest men's champion in history.

Becker's first win was the most remarkable. Before the 1985 tournament began, no one thought Becker had a chance. He was not even one of the top sixteen ranked men's players that year. In fact, gamblers in London set the odds against Becker's winning at 10,000 to 1! But the graceful seventeen-year-old defeated opponent after opponent to reach the semifinals and then the finals. Becker's secrets were his amazing quickness on the court and his acrobatics. On several occasions, he was far out of position as the ball came over the net, but he dove along the grass to return the shots for winners. When he triumphed over Kevin Curren for the 1985 title, Becker became the youngest male champion in the history of the All-England Championship.

Both of the players on Centre Court today are hoping to become a part of the Wimbledon tradition. Boris Becker is attempting to win his third championship in five years, and Ivan Lendl hopes to win his first.

Ivan Lendl challenged Becker for the title in 1989.

Their match is grueling and takes nearly four hours to complete. Each player loses up to ten pounds as they run, leap, and even dive to reach the ball and return it over the net. In the end, Becker again wins and takes his place in tennis history alongside such all-time greats as Willie Renshaw, Bill Tilden, Rene Lacoste, Fred Perry, Rod Laver, Bjorn Borg, and John McEnroe. He holds aloft the giant cup that symbolizes the Wimbledon Championship. He shakes the hand of a member of England's royal family and acknowledges the cheers of the thousands of fans crowding the edges of Centre Court. He has survived the "Fabulous Fortnight" and has emerged victorious.

Boris Becker provided another great moment in Wimbledon's history. In his victory speech addressed to the 14,000 fans around Centre Court and the millions more watching on television around the world, he echoes the words of past champion Martina Navratilova: "There's no place I'd rather be, no title I'd rather win."